Diary of
Steve and the
Wimpy Creeper

An Unofficial Minecraft Series

Book 2

Skeleton Steve

www.SkeletonSteve.com

Copyright

"Diary of Steve and the Wimpy Creeper – Book 2"

Published in the United States of America by Lightbringer Media LLC, 2017

To join Skeleton Steve's free mailing list, for updates about new Minecraft Fanfiction titles:

www.SkeletonSteve.com

Table of Contents

Contents

Diary of Steve and the Wimpy Creeper....................

Copyright ....

Table of Contents ....

Book Introduction by Skeleton Steve.................... 1

Day 4.. 9

Day 5.. 25

Day 6.. 51

Day 7.. 77

Night 7 113

Want More Steve and Cree? 143

About the Author - Skeleton Steve 145

Other Books by Skeleton Steve 149

Enjoy the Excerpt from...................................... 161

The Amazing Reader List 185

Book Introduction by Skeleton Steve

Love MINECRAFT? **Over 14,000 words of kid-friendly fun!**

This high-quality fan fiction fantasy diary book is for kids, teens, and nerdy grown-ups who love to read epic stories about their favorite game!

Cree the Creeper ran away!!

After book 1, when Steve introduced his new creeper friend, Cree, to his friends, they scared him away! Now, Steve is determined to find his new friend and bring him back home. But when the search for Cree leads him into a massive and dangerous underground dungeon, will Steve have the strength and resourcefulness to locate Cree and get out alive?

Thank you to <u>all</u> of you who are buying and reading my books and helping me grow as a writer.

I put many hours into writing and preparing this for you. I *love* Minecraft, and writing about it is almost as much fun as playing it. It's because of *you*, reader, that I'm able to keep writing these books for you and others to enjoy.

This book is dedicated to *you*. Enjoy!!

After you read this book, please take a minute to leave a simple review. I really appreciate the feedback from my readers, and love to read your reactions to my stories, good or bad. If you ever want to see your name/handle featured in one of my stories, leave a review and *tell me about it* in there! And if you ever want to ask me any questions, or tell me your idea for a cool Minecraft story, you can email me at steve@skeletonsteve.com.

Are you on my **Amazing Reader List**? Find out at the end of the book!

August 17th, 2016

The story of Steve meeting Cree, the Wimpy Creeper, has been pretty popular, so here's book 2! In the last few weeks, I've been working on Youtube videos and *so many books!* Soon, you guys will see a book about a SLIME, and the first book in a new series about an Enderman Ninja! (I really like that one.)

My books are definitely getting into more hands. Thanks to all of you who have been leaving reviews! You know who you are. :) Keep an eye out for more. And, in case you didn't know, I have a website where you can see all of the books and read free previews.

Enjoy the story.

P.S. - Have you joined the Skeleton Steve Club and my Mailing List?? *Check online to learn how!*

You found one of my diaries!!

Some of these books are my own stories, and some are the tales of the friends I've made along the way. And a precious few of my books, like this one, are from my "Fan Series", which means that it's a book I worked on *together* with one of my fans! Make sure to let me *and the fan who helped me know* if you like our book!

This story is from the *Diamond55* Fan Series. It takes place on a

Minecraft world, much like my own Diamodia, where Steve and his friends call themselves *Minecraftians*.

What you are about to read is the *second* collection of diary entries from Steve the Minecraftian, about his adventure to find his new creeper friend, Cree, after Alex and his other friends scared the friendly mob away!

*Note: This is **Book 2** in a Series!*

If you're new to this series, you'll want to read the previous books before you read this one, or the story won't make sense!

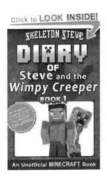

Be warned—this is an *epic book!* You're going to *care* about these characters. You'll be scared for them, feel good for them, and feel bad for them! It's my hope that you'll be *sucked up* into the story, and the adventure and danger will be so intense, you'll forget we started this journey with a *video game!*

With that, readers, I present to you the tale of **Steve and the Wimpy Creeper**, Book 2...

Day 4

Well, we have some serious problems!

Aaaahhhh!

What crazy stuff I've gotten into since I let a creeper into my home! What ever happened to my easy, simple little life??

Sigh.

Let me start over.

So ... yesterday, Cree, Alex and the gang all *met*.

I was super excited, but when Alex saw him, I realized that maybe this wasn't such a good idea...

My friend became really hostile toward Cree, and it really made me sad to think that my friends wouldn't be able to see past his creeper exterior.

I mean—Cree wasn't just a creeper!

He was my *best friend!*

Alex was really mad at me for endangering myself like this, and she wouldn't lower her weapon even *after* I asked her to. Cree became really *scared*, since he wasn't used to anyone being so threatening towards him, and he *ran away!*

That's right!

My current best friend scared off my *new* best friend! It was a super lousy feeling...

After that, Alex and I got into a really bad argument. It wasn't about her not accepting a *creeper* into our group—it was that she didn't even want to give Cree, my friend, a chance to show her who he was!

It just wasn't *fair!*

She and the other Minecraftians left a after a little while, and I was *very worried* about Cree. The last time he ran off, I went out to get him. This time, I had no idea where he might have gone, because of how scared he was.

"Pfft, he's probably going to the dungeon at the foot of the mountain,"

Alex had shouted at me before she left.

She did that to upset me.

Alex *knew* that I didn't like dungeons or anything monster-related!

"Whatever!" I shouted back, but part of me knew that she was probably right. My heart dropped at the thought of what I knew I had to do. "Wait! Alex! Where is it?!"

I didn't want to go to a dungeon.

I *really* didn't want to go!

Alex told me how to get there and she seemed to laugh at me, as if she didn't believe that I would take the risk to get out there. One final glance at her, then back at the mountains, and I took a deep breath.

I knew what I had to do.

With my armor ready, weapons on, and super-determined, I traveled to the foot of the mountain over most of the day.

Dungeons are normally pretty small, so the others tell me. They're apparently like a small room with a monster spawner and some treasure. I've never actually seen one.

But, according to Alex, the dungeon in the mountain was 'extra large'—whatever that meant. I guess I was going to see for myself.

"It's alright, man," I told myself. "You know there's a monster spawner. You know what to expect. Be cool. You can handle this..."

There is really no describing how *terrified* I was to go alone on this adventure, but Cree needed me, and I was not going to let him down!

Later in the day, the mountain loomed over me, casting a long and heavy shadow over all of the surrounding foothills. It was enormous! My neck craned all the way back just to try to spy the peak of it, and even still, I couldn't see the very top!

Uh oh! It was getting dark, and fast!

Soon, there would be monsters everywhere! I could already hear the moans and bustling of some zombies stirring awake. In a panic, I ran behind the nearest tree, shaking and hoping that they went away!

As we have established by now, I never make a whole lot of sense when in a *panic* situation. Obviously, hiding behind a tree when there were zombies stumbling around through the forest was *not the best idea!* But for a few seconds, I felt completely safe!

I thought to myself, *you know, Steve, this is actually a bad idea.*

So I looked around for materials to make myself a house. It didn't need to be huge or super-*fortified*, it just needed to hold out the night.

A *hut*, really.

First, I had to strategically plan out my little house.

I wanted to build it somewhere that was as protected as possible to start with. It wasn't going to be very strong, wasn't going to have massive walls or moats or anything, but I knew I could do *something*...

After scouting the area, I decided the best place to build my *hut* was up against the foot of the mountain. This way, the back of my house was against one of the most solid structures in all of creation!

"Good plan, Steve!" I said to myself, "Good plan!"

Zombie footsteps nearby pulled me out of my daydreams.

"Okay!" I said. "Enough planning!"

After scanning my inventory, I decided that I would use my stone tools to dig up some cobblestone, to build a relatively *sturdy* house. Sturdier than *dirt*, anyway.

It was going to be a simple structure, with one room and a door. I also decided not to use any of my diamond gear. There was no sense in wasting them on dirt and rock! I pulled out my backup shovel and pickaxe, made of stone.

I had to work quickly!

The mobs were coming. I could hear the *grrrs* and *hssssssss's* of all the monsters...

Placing cobblestone blocks down, I built a foundation a few stones deep, then built the walls up. I put on a crude roof, a door, plopped a torch onto the wall, and figured I was done.

There. Small, but effective.

I could barely fit into the structure standing, and had to sit to be comfortable, but it was *perfect!* My little hut wouldn't attract too much attention. Hopefully, the monsters would pass it up as they *grrr-ed* and *hssss-ed* their way around the mountain.

The first hour of the night in the hut was the hardest.

Every single noise that came from outside made me nearly jump out of my armor in terror! Every *crack*, *snap*, and *chirp* put me over the edge. I sat with my back against the wall of the mountain, watching the door with an intensity that almost made my head hurt.

"They're right out there! I know it!" I muttered to myself.

Looking back now, I realize that I was being *extremely* paranoid!

You can't blame me, though! It was scary, dark, and there were *tons* of monsters out there! *You* wouldn't have been able to sleep either!

I tried to sleep, but I just couldn't...

About half way through the night I must have passed out, because I was suddenly startled awake by a zombie bashing on my door! My heart almost stopped!

I didn't move—I didn't even breathe!

After a little while, the undead mob seemed to lose interest, and it just walked away.

I didn't sleep *at all* after that.

For the rest of the night, my eyes were completely *glued* to the door, which I knew would be broken down *any minute now...*

Day 5

That 'any minute now' never came, thankfully, and before I knew it, the sun was up and the monsters were all leaving to seek shelter! I was initially extremely happy until it dawned on me that I was right outside of a dungeon.

The odds were pretty good that the monsters from last night all spawned *in* the dungeon and were most likely going *back* into the dungeon for the day!

The dungeon that I was about to go into myself...

"Great. Just great..."

This was not going to be fun for me.

I waited a little longer than I needed to before coming out of my shelter, and looked into the mouth of the cave. A chill ran through my body, and I immediately stiffened in fear. This was *not* going to be the easiest thing in the world.

But I could do it.

I had to.

"You just spent an entire night in a *shack!* You can do this! You can do this, Steve!" I pumped myself up as I paced back and forth outside of the hut. I must have looked like a crazy person.

I jumped in place for a bit to get my energy going, and looked up at the looming mountain again.

"You're not going to scare me! *Cree* is in there! And I'm going for him!"

With my eyes closed and my sword out, I bolted into the den of darkness before I could change my mind!

Immediately, I noticed the change in the air. It was much cooler in here than it was outside. The cave air was also humid, and I could feel the darkness pressing in on me.

A very *creepy-crawly* sort of feeling made me shiver.

I wouldn't stop though! I wasn't going to stop until I was too far in there to chicken out!

I wasn't entirely sure what I was thinking, but for some reason, in my mind, I imagined that the dungeon would just be inside the mouth of the cave. *Let's just walk up to the mountain, step into the dungeon, then step out again! Easy-peasy!*

Thinking ahead to this moment, I never figured that I would have to *look for it* or anything...

So I was a little surprised when I realized that I was going through a maze of stone tunnels, didn't know where I was going, and had no concept of where I would end up!

After a few more minutes of turning left, then right, and *left again*, I stopped, and decided to strategize about how to best accomplish this task.

"Okay!" I said to myself, my voice echoing in the dark, stone cavern. "Let's list out what you came here to do, Steve!

"Goal #1 – Find the dungeon inside the mountain.

Goal #2 – Find Cree and bring him home.

Obstacle #1 – Don't know where the dungeon is.

Obstacle #2 – Lots of monsters."

I nodded to myself to reinforce this. "I can do it!"

The dungeon is at the heart of the caves beneath the mountain. That's what Alex had said...

"If I keep walking, I should be able to find it. I just need to go ... this way?"

What started out as wandering turned into strategized movements into the depths of the stone monster. I figured that if I was going to wander around, I may as well wander into the central depths of the giant structure.

Keep moving forward. Keep moving down.

The tunnels became impossibly dark.

Never in my life had I imagined that there was a level of darkness as intense and as solid as the one that lingered past the end of my torch!

Have *you* ever been deep underground?? It's a special kind of dark. Black like you wouldn't believe!

I had to be careful not to use up the torches I brought for the dungeon. So I resisted the temptation to use them to make a path behind me, even though that would have really helped in getting back out.

As I pressed on, the darkness seemed to *slither* out of the way of the light. The shadows looked very slow and almost alive. My skin crawled under my armor out of fear.

The tunnel walls were narrow, not very tall, and I had to slump down sometimes to make it into another passage of the maze.

"I have to be getting there soon," I said, feeling very small.

I had no clue how long I'd been walking those dark and lonely tunnels. It seemed like *forever!*

"Why are there no monsters?" I asked, aloud.

Not that I was *complaining*, but it was strange that I hadn't encountered any mobs this far into the caverns!

There was a very low entrance coming up and it required me to squat down and crawl through the opening. I put my torch away, making sure that I was in the clear before trying to jump. I landed with a loud and heavy *thump* and winced at the how loud it was. The dull sound echoed throughout the maze and immediately attracted something's attention.

I could hear it, moving toward me. Panic began to take over my body, and my shaking hands refused to open up my inventory and take out a torch to at least *see* what it was!

"*Sssss. Rrrrrr,*" something said in the dark.

What kind of monster made *those* noises?!

"Come on! Come on!" I stammered at myself.

"*Mmmmmrrrrrr,*" the creature said, very close to me.

Zombie. It had to be a zombie. I had no way of confirming though, since my torch refused to light!

Suddenly, everything went quiet. My movement stopped. I stood as still as I possibly could, fighting with my body's desire to tremble. Then, without any warning, the sound came again.

"*Rrrrr!*" the zombie said *right next to me*.

"Aaaahhh!" I yelled in surprise.

My armor almost *flew* off of me from how fast I sprinted away. The monster had been right *behind* me!

Behind me?! *Yes!*

Somehow, I had missed an opening somewhere, and the mob had crept up on me from *under* the level I was standing on. I could still hear it behind me, *grrr-ing* and *sssrr-ing*. The more I ran, the further away the sound was.

Stomp, stomp, stomp, stomp!

The heavy armor made my footsteps sound louder and heavier than they normally did. Before I could decide that I didn't need to run anymore, the decision was made for me. Just as I was about to stop, my foot moved into the air, and when it came down to set on the ground, my heart flew out of my chest when I realized that there was absolutely *nothing there!*

"Aaaahhh!" I screamed.

The speed I was running pushed the rest of my body forward and into the empty space. There was nothing to catch me or grab onto.

Only darkness.

I plummeted into the unknown.

"I'm going to die!" I cried.

That's all I was able to yell before I landed on my side, with a crash and the sound of breaking glass...

I must have knocked myself out, because when I awoke later, I couldn't tell which direction I was facing, or where I was! I was waiting for the pain to rise up and tell me that I wouldn't be able to move...

But the pain didn't come.

When nothing happened, I opened my eyes and looked around.

Well, I *tried* to look around. I still couldn't see anything because of how dark the caves were, but I sure was happy to be alive!

Whatever monster was pursuing me in the tunnels above hadn't followed me down. I slowly stood up. I was still surprised that I hadn't *died*. I didn't even break anything!

The tunnel I fell into was bigger than the last one. I couldn't feel any of the walls around me, and after rooting around in my inventory for a while, I lit a torch.

The walls around me, I immediately noticed, were not the raw stone of a natural cave. I reached out to touch them, and realized that they were mossy cobblestone—green and dank with growth.

"Huh ... that's weird," I said to myself. "Most caves don't have moss stone."

A light at the end of the very long tunnel caught my attention.

There was nothing behind me but more wall, and nothing under me or around me of interest. The only opening I could see was the opening with the light, up ahead. I put out my torch and made my way toward the glow.

Creeping up to the opening, I lied low. My belly grazed the surface of the moss stone below me and I *craned* my neck around the corner of the opening to see if the coast was clear. What I saw completely shocked me...

There, right before my eyes, was the dungeon!

It must have been.

The tunnels were *enormous*! So much bigger than the tiny, skinny caverns I was wandering through to get here! There were chains and gates all around. Silverfish slithered away from me. I hadn't even noticed them until now!

My body crashed against the wall as I jumped up and away from the little monsters. Even as small as they were, those silverfish could seriously hurt me! And I didn't have time for that! I needed to find Cree and bring him home!

A sense of relief washed over me when I realized that one goal of my mission had been achieved.

I found the dungeon!

Okay, well, 'found' was maybe a strong word to use. It was more I *fell and stumbled* into the dungeon, but the point of it all was that I was here!

Finally!

"Alright! Good job, Steve!" I said to myself, my voice echoing in the large tunnel. "Good job!"

Yes, I was *extremely* proud of myself. But now that I was here, I didn't really know what to do!

I laughed. I'm not the best planner I guess.

"That's alright! That's alright!" I said to myself. I didn't want to feel like I'd come all this way for nothing! "Plan it out! Gotta *strategize*, Steve, just like last time!"

I heard the moan of a zombie from around a corner, and clamped my hands over my mouth.

I needed to be more quiet! If I tipped off the monsters to my presence, I'd be fighting every mob in here!

So, I thought for a while, then knew what to do.

First, I'd put down some kind of trail of markers—a way to find my way back out. That was why I brought the torches with me!

Then, I would go deep into the dungeon, always following a path to the *right,* until I either found Cree … or a dead end. Then the next tunnel— there were several. Rinse, repeat. I don't know why I chose the *right* tunnel first—it didn't really make any difference, so one was as good as another.

As I crept into the dark, imposing complex, I set up a torch every several steps. Every now and again, I looked back to make sure that my torches weren't being taken down.

By whom? I thought. *Who would take down my torches?* I didn't know—I just wanted to make sure that I didn't have anything following me!

Although the tunnels were enormous, I still felt a little cramped and claustrophobic. It felt like the walls were pressing in on me. The humidity radiating off the moss stone made me sweat as I moved deeper into the dungeon...

Day 6

I don't know how long I'd been down here, but I kept going. Nothing was going to stop me. I had to find Cree, no matter what!

Not all of the tunnels and passages were lit. Some were, and had torches lining the walls haphazardly, put up randomly and abandoned.

The tunnel I was in right now, however, was dark. There were sections of the path that ended in darkened pods. I *really* didn't want to go in there, afraid that a monster would jump out at me.

But the fact that Cree might be in one of them made me pause.

Argh!

Sometimes, when I was tired, I would go into one of these little pods to rest after making sure that it was clear.

To set up a quick safe place for a nap, first, I would barricade the door with some stone that I still had left over, then I would settle in for a little shuteye.

But I knew that I couldn't stay too long—I'd get caught!

I checked almost every single empty room I passed, just in case. I didn't want to miss the *one* room that Cree could be in.

Sometimes, I heard footsteps and moans inside, so I passed around the occupied rooms and pods with monsters inside as quietly as I could.

After all this time, I was still undetected. *Amazing!*

I was going to have a heart attack down here—I knew it!

For some reason, another room I passed felt a little … different. I couldn't quite put my finger on it, but I listened to my gut and approached more slowly.

I crept up to the entry. First my forehead peaked around the wall, then my eyes and finally my nose.

Immediately, I began to shake. There was something moving in there and it was *huge*. Oh no! Oh no! This was exactly what I was afraid of!

That wasn't Cree.

I knew Cree's shape and size, and this thing was *much* bigger than he was.

My hands began to shake and I held my breath to keep my armor from clattering. My teeth started chattering, so I gulped down the fear in my throat and tried to keep my cool...

In the room ahead of me, a few feet away from my face, was a *giant* spider.

The entire room was covered in enormous, sticky webs. The long strings glistened against the torch light. An enormous spider sat at the very center of the web, waiting for prey to stumble into its clutches.

That prey would have been *me*, if something in my gut hadn't told me to approach with *extreme* caution.

It twitched, turning its head, as if the sound of my armor made it perk up in attention. Its four glowing red eyes scanned the darkness.

My breathing stopped, and I slowly walked away, not once taking my eyes off the entrance to the room, just in case the spider decided to come after me. I could still make a dash for it if the creepy-crawly monster gave chase.

After a few minutes of walking backwards and trying to calm myself, I finally turned around.

Phew! That was a close one!

I could have been eaten by that giant spider, and that would have been that! No home, or Cree, or *anything!*

The end.

I shook my head to clear out the fear that made my brain feel like a fog. Now was not the time for this sort of nonsense.

I kept walking deeper into the dungeon until I finally came upon the monster spawner at the structure's cobblestone heart.

Skeleton bones clanked and clattered in the dark.

Great.

Skeletons. *Eeewgh! Gross!* I *hate* skeletons! No wonder there are so many skeletons around my home!

"On the bright side," I said to myself, "at least you're in the center of the dungeon!"

Next to where I was standing, near the entrance to the monster-spawner room, a chest sat up against the wall. I hoped that there would be something useful inside!

The mobs were far enough away—maybe I could reach the chest without the skeletons noticing!

Creeping over and quietly opening the wooden containers, I found some bones, bread, and rotten flesh. It was practically empty.

Hmmmm. Not the worst, but not the best.

At least there was some bread. I was starving! I hadn't even noticed my hunger until I smelled the old food. I grabbed the loaf, and ate the entire thing there in the dungeon, keeping my eye on the skeletons walking around not far from me.

How had I been so hungry and not noticed it?! Fear is a powerful thing, let me tell you. It really does override all of your other senses!

The monster spawner flashed in the darkness suddenly, and in a puff of smoke, another skeleton appeared near the others.

It occurred to me that this chest with bread and mob junk in it might be the first chest I'd ever opened outside of the village.

What a sheltered life I've lived! I bet if Alex and the others were here, they wouldn't be sneaking around. They'd just kill everything and make the dungeon safe.

As I ate the bread and pondered, I noticed a corridor going off into the darkness near me that was shaped differently than the rest of the dungeon.

How odd. Did my friends carve into the wall there in the past?

After I finished eating the loaf, something in my gut told me that *that* was the way I wanted to go...

I decided to listen to my instincts for a change.

Now, keep in mind, this entire time I'd been putting my torches up on the walls to make sure that I could find my way back. So *la de daa*, there I went putting up my torches willy-nilly, and then I realized with surprise ... there was only one torch left!

"What?!"

My voice echoed through the dark halls.

Out of torches!

I ran back the way I came to take some of my other torches off of the walls, trying to space them out more wisely.

"No! I thought I packed more!"

A skeleton clattered somewhere.

Well, turns out I hadn't. I was going through a monster-infested dungeon, looking for Cree, and now I was almost completely out of torches!

"Great! Just great, Steve!"

I wished I paid more attention up until now, so that I could have divided up the torches better. I had a *whole chest* full of coal back home! But there was nothing I could do about it now.

I looked down the hall. Man, it was *long!*

"Okay, this hall is pretty long ... *but* ... it's probably a dead end!" I whispered to myself. "First, down this hall and then *back*, and you'll have torches again! Brilliant, Steve! Brilliant!"

Slowly, I made my way down the hall.

Knowing that I had only a few torches remaining made me even more afraid of my surroundings, even though the monsters were behind me.

In the pit of my stomach, I felt that this was going to end badly. Somehow, I just *knew* that something bad was going to happen. But I kept going, because *honestly*, in a dark and monster-infested dungeon, things were *already* bad!

I hung my last torch. I wouldn't have enough to make it all the way to the end of the corridor. I'd have to walk the end of it in the dark.

Without a torch to distract me, I wrung my hands together.

"Still hidden," I told myself. "Almost at the end. Almost there, Steve!"

I could almost see the dark outline of the end wall but something in me told me to keep going. *Slower and slower, just a little more,* I thought. Then it turned into … nope! Turning back!

But I tried to hold out as long as I could. I tried to keep going with my dimming light behind me, barely able to see in the darkness.

By the time I panicked and turned back, I was almost crawling to stay low and avoid being seen by whatever was at the end of this tunnel.

I couldn't do it. I just couldn't. I started back for the last torch I hung on the wall, and felt the guilt hit me.

I had let Cree down.

For some reason, not going to the end of the hallway felt like the worst thing I could have done. It felt like I had just abandoned Cree for some reason, while I crawled back the way I came. This time, however, I didn't crawl away out of fear. I slunk through the corridor, hiding in the shadows and taking back my torches, out of shame. I had just abandoned my best friend to this dungeon! I was a terrible person! In my shame, I paused, and that's when I heard it.

"*Grrrr,*" a creature said nearby.

I froze, terrified. What made that sound? I knew I didn't *really* want to know, but I turned around anyway. Why? Because I don't think things through!

As I squinted through the darkness, I could see that there was something down there...

"Grrrrrrrrr."

Yup. There was *definitely* something down there.

"Grrr." Over in the dark. Sounded familiar.

I felt frozen. I saw what it was...

It was a creeper!

"Grrr," it said, and it was on the move.

Coming right at me!

I didn't move. After running away from and running into Cree so many times now, I knew better. I think I learned that not every single creeper was dangerous.

At least, I *hoped* that this was the case!

The approaching creeper might have been Cree!

I really need to give him a necklace or something so I can tell which one he is, I thought to myself.

I shook my head. Why hadn't I thought of that idea sooner? Well, I'd only known Cree for almost a week now, and I don't really prepare too far ahead for bad things to happen!

Mental Note: Prepare for bad things to happen!

Closer and closer the creeper came. Slowly. The mob didn't seem to be in a rush—didn't seem dead set on blowing me up or anything—so I decided that I needed to take a chance.

"Cree?"

If this creeper wasn't Cree, I was in *big* trouble!

It paused and looked at me.

The monster appeared almost completely *black* in the dark, and for one dreadful moment, I didn't think it was Cree. Its sad, black eyes peered at me, looked through me, looked at the hallway behind me...

This was it! I was going to be blown away by a creeper! Again!

Although it was a terrible thing, I didn't feel too bad about how everything was all going to end for me. I had done my very best to find Cree, and if I was going to meet my end like this, I was going to die as a hero!

Not too bad for someone who was afraid of monsters...

I backed away, then fell backwards to the floor. The creeper kept coming, so I began to crawl backwards. Not too fast! I didn't want to trigger an explosion!

The mob paused and looked at me. Oh no! It was going to explode! I don't know why but instead of running away in that pause I just sat there, frozen. It shook its head, then looked at me with more intensity.

This is it!

The creeper jumped at me.

"Aaaaahh!" I screamed.

Thump!

The monster landed on top me and stared down at my pale and horrified face. He didn't explode.

"Cree?!"

I could swear the creeper's frown twisted into a subtle smile...

Day 7

His head rubbed against my helmet and I rolled over, tossing him off my body.

"Cree! It *is* you! Oh my *gosh!* You're alive!"

I hugged him close to me and he *grr-ed* and *hissed* with joy.

"Do you *like* giving me heart attacks?!"

"*Grrrrr. Hisssss!*" he said.

"I'll take that as a yes!" I exclaimed, laughing.

Cree seemed to almost be laughing with me. I couldn't believe I had found him! Actually, *he* had found *me*! What were the odds??

I put my hand where his shoulder would have been and smiled.

"Cree, let's go home!"

We both stood, and were about to go back up the tunnel, back to the monster spawn room, when Cree stood in my way.

"Hey, what's going on?"

He moved backwards, not looking at me as he pushed me backwards with his leafy body—back toward the end of the tunnel.

Oh no. This was bad.

At first, I was very confused, but I knew Cree well enough by now to know that if he was doing this, then it was for a good reason!

As quietly as possible, I darted back to the dead end and made myself as small as I could be. Cree came running behind me and he pushed me into the corner of the room.

He purred at me, as if telling me to stay put.

I nodded, and became a quiet bundle of cloth and armor behind him. Cree stood in front of me, crushing his back against me to try to cover my shiny armor with his green and grassy body.

I heard the clicking before I saw the monster. A skeleton appeared further down the long hallway and looked around, as if trying to find a wayward Minecraftian—a squishy, warm-fleshed Minecraftian who had been shouting and making a ruckus in the tunnel...

Keeping my head down, afraid that if I looked at the skeleton, I would attract his attention, I quietly berated myself for being so loud and dumb!

What was I thinking, causing such commotion in a monster-infested dungeon!? It's a *wonder* I wasn't discovered until now!

The skeleton looked around a little more. Was it trying to decide if he could trust Cree enough to truly be alone in the room?

Cree did not move an inch. He stood tall and protective over me, and I knew that if the skeleton attacked, then Cree would take the full brunt of it to save me.

Please don't attack! Please don't attack! I thought.

I couldn't stand to think that Cree would get hurt trying to save me ... again!

The skeleton archer turned around a few times, as if confused, then walked back down the tunnel. It seemed to have lost interest, but Cree still did not move out from in front of me. He wanted to make sure that the skeleton was really gone before moving.

I didn't budge.

My friend was so much smarter than I had originally thought! Cree really was the *best* friend I could ever ask for.

After Cree was satisfied that the skeleton had gone off on his scary way, he moved and motioned with his head for me to follow him out. I nodded in silence and crept out behind him.

I had learned my lesson! Don't be too loud when there were monsters waiting to get you!

Cree lead the way out of the room and the long hallway, and when he noticed the trail torches I left, he looked up in confusion.

"Oh yeah," I chuckled. "That was me. So we could find our way back out…"

"*Grrrr*," he said.

I wonder what he meant.

Moving over to the lit-up wall, I began taking the torches down, one by one, as we crept along side by side.

At first, everything was going well. The torches were coming down and there wasn't a monster in sight.

Then I heard something and froze…

"Sssh." I said, putting a hand on Cree. "Don't move." I took down the nearest torch and stopped.

My friend must have heard the sound too. Cree had his expressions, as subtle as they were, and I knew that he had heard the sound, too.

There was something behind us.

We moved forward a little more, then stopped.

"*Grrrrr. Rrrrr.*" Cree said.

I looked over at the sound he just made, and realized that Cree wasn't there. He was up ahead just a little.

"Did you say that?" I asked.

Cree shook his head, making a sound like rustling leaves.

Maybe it's all in your head, Steve!

After a few more steps, we paused again.

"*Rrrrrgh,*" something said. It was a deep, rumbly voice.

Not Cree.

Yup. There was *definitely* something behind us!

I began to panic, fumbling with the torches I was still trying to take down. The monster following behind us wasn't just keeping pace—it was faster, and *gaining* on us.

Much faster!

This was bad! This was very bad! A look at Cree, and I think he felt it was really bad too!

"Grrrrrr!" Cree said, his dark eyes wide.

"I agree! Run!!"

We both sprinted off as fast as we could!

My armor was loud and noisy. Cree was soft and swift, his clawed little legs almost flying over the moss stone. Man! I needed to become more agile! There was no time for that right now, though! We were being chased! And we had to make it home! I didn't bother to take the rest of the torches, as we rushed down the tunnel. They guided us out of the maze of tunnels and that was *fine by me!* That's all we needed!

Home! We have to make it home!

I listened behind us, trying to hear over the *clank* of my armor and my flying footsteps.

The monster was still coming after us!

Whatever it was, it wasn't going to stop just because of a few torches. I looked at Cree and I felt he might be thinking the same thing.

Neither of us looked back. We focused on the tunnels winding in front of us and trying to see far enough ahead to know which way the torches turned. The last thing we wanted was to have to slow down to *think* about which way to go with this *thing* chasing us.

I started to hear the sounds of other mobs stirring all around us.

We bolted through the monster spawner room, and the skeletons in the room, hanging out around the spawning cage, startled at our explosive entrance.

It gave us a few seconds to get past them before they raised their bows and came after us.

"Grrr. Grrr! Hissss!" Cree exclaimed.

What? I don't know what he was—

I suddenly tripped on the corner of the wooden chest.

Clank! Thunk! Oomph!

I stumbled over myself trying to recover, but managed to keep running. Now was *not* the time! A couple of arrows *thunked* into the cobblestone wall next to my head.

"Aaaahhh!"

We ran past all of the darkened pod rooms.

The giant spider emerged with a ferocious *hissssss*, its long legs stretching out into the hall. I jumped over them and kept going.

"Cree! Keep running!"

The mob behind us sounded bigger and faster than us!

And now it was being joined with everything else in this huge dungeon!

Raaaarrrrr!

And it definitely did not sound very happy. A zombie? No, it was running way too fast for that but I was *not* going to stop to check!

I was getting tired. How long had we been running? This dungeon was a lot bigger than it seemed when I was taking my time through it before.

Finally!

Up ahead I saw the first torch I had put down upon entering the dungeon. We were almost there.

"Cree! We're almost there! Don't stop!"

But Cree was fine. It wasn't Cree that was growing tired—it was me. I felt exhausted at the worst possible time!

No, no, no! The bread was gone, and I had no food!

Again, I had forgotten to bring food on an adventure with me! Not like I could imagine eating on the run, but I would have felt better if I had it, at least!

Looking behind us, into the huge, tall, and wide hall of moss-covered cobblestone, I saw the shadows of monsters stretching in the torchlight from behind us. Grinning skeletons and other shapes, full of elongated claws, weapons, and other pointy bits.

"Gotta make it all the way," I gasped at myself, as I felt my energy dwindling.

I had to make it! I hadn't come this far to stop before I was home!

You can do it! You can do it!

The voice in my head was desperate.

However, even as I told myself this, I saw an obstacle ahead that made my heart lurch.

A wall. A completely solid cobblestone wall.

We both stopped. This could not be the way in. Had we taken a wrong turn somewhere!? No! No! We had followed the torches I had set correctly! I saw them all! Had I messed up somewhere? Oh no!

I could see the torchlight glittering on some broken glass. What was that?

Cree looked back at the group of mobs closing in on us and growled menacingly. There behind us, not far now, was the giant dark form that had been chasing us all this time! It didn't even register to me what it was. The torchlight behind it cast its features into shadows, and all I saw was a huge, scary creature, running at us very, *very* fast!

"Calm down Steve! Calm down!" I shouted at myself.

This was the entrance! I knew that much! Now, we just had to find the *exit*. How had I gotten in?! I looked down at the broken glass again, then my eyes went up to a small hole in the wall, and I remembered how I got in.

I hadn't *walked* in! A monster had chased me and I had *fallen* into the dungeon!

Running over to the broken glass, I saw that it was the remains of a shattered glass vial. There was a piece of paper, still attached to some tiny pieces of glass. It was a label.

I picked it up and looked at it.

"Invisibility"
Alex

What??

One of Alex's Invisibility potions? What's it doing here? Is that what I broke when I fell?

I stuffed the label into my inventory, then looked back to the hole in the wall.

Oh no.

The wall was too tall. We weren't going to be able to make it up. I looked into my inventory again, trying to stay as calm as possible, trying to *not panic,* and to my surprise, I found some meat!

I quickly inhaled the food but did not find any stone or wood or sand. There was nothing I could use make some steps or a ladder. I had used everything I dug up earlier to make the hut.

The monster was just a few paces away. In a few seconds, it would attack us, and we would both die.

Cree hissed and growled at the monster, pushing me into the corner. He was covering me with himself again. My friend was going to defend me, even though it was going to be my fault that we died

I looked down at the ground, sad and disappointed...

No!

It wasn't going to end like this!

Cree and I would fight together! And we would be able to defeat this bizarre monster!

Cree kept shoving me back into the corner and I readied myself for the battle of my life. But just when I was

103

about to draw my sword and turn around, I saw the answer!

There was another opening. Another hole in the wall. But this was a small opening *under* the wall! This was it! This was our way out.

I punched at the floor, trying to break away one more block! Just *one block*, and both Cree and I would be able to fit through it. We would make it! On the other side, I saw a dark void. An unknown hole that would lead us to who-knows-where, but it would be away from the monsters!

Come on! Come on!

Thump! Thump! Thump!

It wasn't breaking, but I kept punching! Nothing was going to stop me now! I had to save us!

Thump! Thump! Crack!

Aha! It was broken!

I turned around, wrapped my arms around Cree and with *all* of my strength, I *yanked* him backwards with me through the hole. I didn't know how long we were going to fall, but any chance falling into darkness was better than no chance fighting against that enormous monster!

We slipped through with a *plop*, and I heard the loud *thud* of the monster smashing into the wall where were just standing.

About six feet below, Cree and I lay frozen stiff in the darkness, both wondering if we had somehow made it…

The cave we fell into was dark. We couldn't see a thing!

The monster roared above us, and scratched at the walls and the hole I made in the floor with its claws. It was too big to get to us, but the other mobs could probably fit through, just like we did.

We had to hurry. Once the monster backed away from the hole, the skeletons and other mobs might move in.

"Don't worry Cree. I've got this," I said.

From out of my dwindling inventory, I pulled one of the handful of torches I recovered before we fled the dungeon.

It didn't light up much of our surroundings, but it was enough to see that we had fallen into a giant underground room of sorts.

Not a cave. A room. Another section of the dungeon?

Pitch black and quiet.

Huh, weird, I thought.

We couldn't stand all the way so we hunched a bit and walked in the direction of the mountain cave's entrance, passing under the tall wall that was previously in our way.

"If we had gotten through that wall," I explained to Cree, "we would have continued this way. So the exit is this way . . . I hope . . ."

I'm not sure how long we walked through the darkness, tunnel after tunnel. The maze seemed *insane*, too crazy to be real. I thought about pulling out my diamond pickaxe to just start making a bee-line through the walls, but as long as the maze kept going in the direction we needed to go, I didn't want to risk breaking through into anything more dangerous.

We were up the creek without a paddle, but we were going to make it through this crazy day!

Night? Day?

To be honest, I wasn't sure what time it was. All I knew was that we needed to get home as soon as possible!

Eventually, the cobblestone stopped, and we were walking

through stone cave tunnels once again. It was entirely possible that the tunnel we were in at some point connected with the cave tunnels I had already traveled through before, but it all looked the same, and I couldn't tell.

"There! Look!"

"*Grrrrr!*" Cree said.

Cree looked in the direction my torch was pointing and we both felt overjoyed.

There, just a little ways ahead, were stars.

Night 7

We came out of the caves with grins on our faces. A smile sure looked weird on a creeper's face. Neither of us were sure—was it really over?

Had we *really* just survived through all of that??

Were we really okay?!

Somehow, against the odds, we were here, standing in the cool night air in front of the mountain.

I looked around, trying to orient myself, when I saw ... my shack! It was just on the other side of some trees!

"Cree! Look! My hut! I know how to get home!"

"*Grrrr?*" he asked.

"Yeah ... this was where I stayed the night before I went into the caves! I didn't want to go in during the night," I explained.

Cree spun to face me, his expression ... angry? He thwacked my with his head. *Thud!*

"Grrr!" he exclaimed. I could only assume he was mad because ... maybe because I put myself in danger? He hit me again. And again.

"Ow! Hey! *Stop it!* I had to go get you!" I cried.

Cree lightened up his attacks, and started shoving my shoulder with his head.

"Hey! Come on! Look, we *made* it, so everything is okay! Just don't run off anymore!"

"Rrrrrr," Cree groaned.

"It wasn't all my fault that we're here, you know..." I told him.

Cree slumped down a bit, and stopped pushing. He knew.

"It's alright. We're fine. Just don't do it again," I said, then smiled at him.

"*Rrrrrr.*"

"Now, how do we get home...?"

I paused. Did I hear something?

"Steve!" a voice called out.

"Where are you!?" another yelled.

"What? Cree, did you hear that?" I said, listening to the shout of my name. Somewhere ... over the hill, behind us...

"*Grrrrr,*"Cree said.

Alex! It was Alex and the others! I perked up and shouted back to them.

"Alex! Hey! I'm over here!"

"Steve!" another voice cried. It sounded like Mel, another one of my friends. "Hey guys, he's over here! Alex! He's over here!"

Through the darkness I could see small lights bobbing around and coming our way. I couldn't believe it. There, running toward us in the dark, were my friends! Alex sprinted in front, and I could tell who she was even at this distance from the shape of her armor and her hair.

They closed the distance, and Alex tackled me to the ground.

"You psycho!" she shouted as I tried to throw her off of me. "How could you be so dumb?!"

"Ow! Hey!" I covered myself as she shoved me in anger.

"Did you even think this through, Steve?! What if something happened to you?" she cried.

"Grrrr!" Cree growled, and moved to get between us. I stopped him with my hand.

"No, Cree! You're fine!" I said, then turned back to Alex. "Get off me!"

She was sitting on me and had me pinned to the ground, and I tried without success to push her off of me. I was still trying to free myself as Mel and Jack approached.

She punched me in the hip, then climbed off.

"Ow!!" I cried.

She would have probably just punched me in the shoulder, but I was wearing my diamond armor, so she had to find a spot where I was vulnerable. I stood up and dusted myself off as the rest of the gang came around us.

"What are you guys doing here?" I asked. My mind was still racing, and I haven't recovered from the shock that Cree and I had survived the dungeon. And now I was swarmed with my friends out in the middle of nowhere in the middle of the night.

"What do you think?" Alex asked with a huff. "We came out looking for you, dummy! We knew you'd come out this way and when we saw your hut we started looking around. That's when you popped out of the mountain!"

"I was actually here yesterday too," Jack said, sharpening his sword. "I come here every few days to practice fighting. Were there any mobs left?"

What?

"You came looking for me?" I was in total shock.

Is that why the place was so empty?

"Yeah!" Alex was very upset. Even though she's kind of a jerk to me sometimes, I bet she was really worried. "Just because we have a fight over something *dumb* doesn't mean we're not friends anymore! We were going to help you find your friend!"

The rest of the group nodded. She was finally simmering down and relaxing.

"I'm sorry, Alex. I just had to go and get Cree back."

She *humphed* before looking back at me.

"Yeah, I'm sorry too. What a mess we made..."

She walked up to Cree and reached out carefully, petting him on the head. He purred, and leaned into her hand.

"Sorry ... Cree?" she said, trying to remember his name. "We didn't mean to be *jerks* to you! We were just ... surprised! That's all..."

"*Rrrrrrrrrr*," Cree said.

Alex laughed and smiled suddenly, pulling her hand away. "He feels like dry leaves. So weird!"

Everyone laughed.

"*Grrrr*," Cree said.

Alex smiled, then turned back to the creeper. "You're not so bad, Cree. Unlike *him!*" She pointed at me.

"Me?!" I said.

"Yeah, don't ever do that again! You had us so worried!"

"I wasn't worried," Jack said.

Alex glared at him.

I turned to the group. "I'm sorry, everyone. Next time, I'll ask you for help."

"We are friends, you know," Mel said. "Friends do stuff *together*."

Everyone nodded, then took turns apologizing to Cree. Cree *grrrrrr-ed* back his acceptance of their apologies, and we all started the walk back to the village.

It was dark and there were monsters out, but I wasn't afraid.

Everyone had great armor, and everyone but me held their weapons, and cut down any mobs that came too close. I knew we were safe.

"Alex," I said, catching up to her and rifling through my pack.

"Yeah, Steve?" she said.

I pulled out the paper label from the broken flask. There were still small pieces of glass stuck to it. "What's this?" I asked, and handed it to her.

"Oh, that," she said. "Before I left, I put an invisibility potion in your pack. I figured you might run off and do something brash, so I wanted to make sure you at least had a little help..."

"Invisibility potion??" I asked.

"Yep. Did you like it? Get some good use out of it? I had an extra one, and I don't use those much."

"I don't remember ... um ... in my pack? When I fell through the hole ... I ... as in ..." I broke off into muttering as I remembered the flask breaking under me when I fell into the dungeon in the beginning. Then I snuck past all of those monsters...

My face probably turned pale as I felt a flash of fear, and I realized that I was invisible all the way until ... until I found Cree maybe? I thought about the skeletons, and how I was able to sneak past the monster spawner. I was able to get into that chest without being attacked!

All this time, I thought I was just really good at being sneaky!

Was I invisible the *whole time* I was looking for Cree??

I thought about that huge, scary spider. It was listening to my quiet movements, but didn't see me. And I was so close to it! How did it not see my armored head peeking around the doorway?

Because it was looking right *through* me.

I felt a wash of fear go through me, because I realized that if I didn't accidentally make myself invisible by falling on Alex's potion, I would have probably been gobbled up by monsters.

Jeez.

"Uh … Steve?" Alex asked. She waved a hand in front of my face. "You were saying? The potion…?"

"Um … yeah!" I said, snapping back to reality. "I did. Get use out of it. For sure. Thanks!"

We walked quietly for a while. I listened to Cree's quiet, grassy steps behind me, and the clomping of us Minecraftians in our heavy armor.

"He really is that important to you?" Alex asked. "I still can't believe you went into the mountain *by yourself*, and brought him out with you. Not your style, Steve…"

Alex knew how scared I was of monsters.

"He is, yeah," I responded.

Eventually, we saw the village coming up out of the darkness, and I sighed with relief.

I was home. Finally.

After that crazy adventure, I was home.

"*Grrr,*" Cree said, when my house came into view. Did he feel like it was *home* too?

Haha. Correction. *We* were home...

"Thank you all so much for coming to find me and trying to make it right with Cree. It means a lot to me," I told everyone.

"No problem," Mel smiled.

"Put a leash on that thing!" Jack said, then winked. He clapped Cree on the back, and the creeper was jostled, then looked back uncertainly. "Oh, I'm just joshing ya, creeper!" he said, then laughed.

Alex smiled at me. "Steve, you're crazy—you know that?"

I laughed.

Then she got a very dangerous look in her eyes, and I knew that I wasn't going to like it.

"So!" she said. "Since you faced your fears all by yourself, I think it's time you go on an adventure with the rest of us!"

"Yeah! Come on Steve!" Mel said. They all smiled at me.

"What?! Oh, no way!" I said, stammering. "I just got back!" I waved my arms in protest.

"Exactly!" Alex exclaimed. "So rest up, and tomorrow night we go out! That sounds like a plan!"

"But, but … I've got to take care of—"

"Yeah!" Jack cheered. "Steve coming with us on an adventure!"

"Whoo!" Mel said.

"Grrrrr!" Cree exclaimed, trying to smile at the group.

What?! The green, little traitor!

"Cree! No! Really?! You're with *them?!*" I cried.

I couldn't believe Cree!

"Yeah he is!" Alex cheered. "Alright, Cree!" She grinned. "Okay, Steve, so, tomorrow night! It's gonna rock!"

I stood, not knowing what to say, as they all turned to leave, bantering with each other.

136

"Cree," I said. "Really??"

"*Grrrrrrr,*" he said.

"Oh, and Steve!" Alex called, turning around down the street. "Don't forget your *sword* this time!"

Wanna know what happens next??

Continue to the next book in the series!

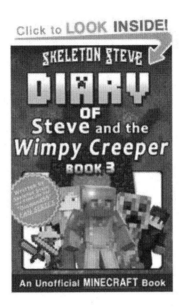

Love MINECRAFT? **Almost 14,000 words of kid-friendly fun!**

This high-quality fan fiction fantasy diary book is for kids, teens, and nerdy grown-ups who love to read epic stories about their favorite game!

Don't PANIC!!

That's what Steve has told himself for years, but it's never stopped him from losing control in stressful situations! But now, Steve and Cree the Creeper are heading off with Steve's friends on his first dangerous adventure. And when the toughest warrior of the group is injured, it's up to Steve and Cree to save the day! Will our wimpy hero be able to find his bravery and rescue his friends?

Love Minecraft adventure??

Read Book 3 of Steve and the Wimpy Creeper now!

CHECK OUT
SKELETONSTEVE.COM
... to find the *NEXT BOOK!*

Sign up for my
Free Newsletter
to get an *email* when
the next book comes out!

Go to: www.SkeletonSteve.com/sub

P.S. ...

This Book Series also has a **BOX SET (Collection)** if you'd rather get a better value and read the series all in one place. *You're gonna read them all anyway. ;)*

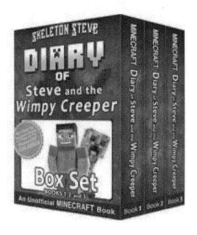

Find the BOX SET Instead!

Save OVER 60% OFF of the Cost of the Books by Themselves
(Also **FREE** on **Kindle Unlimited**)

Want More Steve and Cree?

1. Please go to where you bought this book and *leave a review!* It just takes a minute and it really helps!

2. Join my free *Skeleton Steve Club* and get an email when the next book comes out!

3. Look for your name under my *"Amazing Readers List"* at the end of the book, where I list my *all-star reviewers*. Heck—maybe I'll even use your name in a story if you want me to! (*Let me know in the review!*)

About the Author - Skeleton Steve

I am *Skeleton Steve*, author of *epic* unofficial Minecraft books. *Thanks for reading this book!*

My stories aren't your typical Minecraft junkfood for the brain. I work hard to design great plots and complex characters to take you for a roller coaster ride in their shoes! Er … claws. Monster feet, maybe?

All of my stories written by (just) me are designed for all ages—kind of like the Harry Potter series— and they're twisting journeys of epic adventure! For something more light-hearted, check out my "Fan Series" books, which are collaborations between myself and my fans.

Smart kids will love these books! Teenagers and nerdy grown-ups will have a great time relating with the characters and the stories, getting swept up in the struggles of, say, a novice Enderman ninja (Elias), or the young and naïve creeper king

SKELETON STEVE

(Cth'ka), and even a chicken who refuses to be a zombie knight's battle steed!

I've been *all over* the Minecraft world of Diamodia (and others). As an adventurer and a writer at heart, I *always* chronicle my journeys, and I ask all of the friends I meet along the way to do the same.

Make sure to keep up with my books whenever I publish something new! If you want to know when new books come out, sign up for my mailing list and the *Skeleton Steve Club*. ***It's free!***

Here's my website:
www.SkeletonSteve.com

You can also 'like' me on **Facebook**:
Facebook.com/SkeletonSteveMinecraft

And 'follow' me on **Twitter**:
Twitter.com/SkeletonSteveCo

And watch me on **Youtube**: (Check my website.)

"Subscribe" to my Mailing List and Get Free Updates!

I *love* bringing my Minecraft stories to readers like you, and I hope to one day put out over 100 stories! If you have a cool idea for a Minecraft story, please send me an email at *Steve@SkeletonSteve.com*, and I might make your idea into a real book. I promise I'll write back. :)

Other Books by Skeleton Steve

The "Noob Mob" Books

Books about individual mobs and their adventures becoming heroes of Diamodia.

Diary of Steve and the Wimpy Creeper
Book 2

151

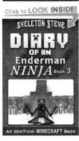

Diary of a Creeper King
Book 1
Book 2
Book 3
Book 4

Diary of Steve and the Wimpy Creeper
Book 2

Skeleton Steve – The Noob Years
Season 1, Episode 1 – **FREE!!**
Season 1, Episode 2
Season 1, Episode 3
Season 1, Episode 4
Season 1, Episode 5
Season 1, Episode 6
Season 2, Episode 1
Season 2, Episode 2
Season 2, Episode 3
Season 2, Episode 4
Season 2, Episode 5
Season 2, Episode 6
Season 2, Episode 6
Season 3, Episode 1
Season 3, Episode 2
Season 3, Episode 3
Season 3, Episode 4
Season 3, Episode 5
Season 3, Episode 6

Diary of a Teenage Zombie Villager
Book 1 – **FREE!!**
Book 2
Book 3
Book 4

Diary of a Chicken Battle Steed
Book 1
Book 2
Book 3
Book 4

SKELETON STEVE

Diary of a Lone Wolf
Book 1
Book 2
Book 3
Book 4

Diary of an Enderman Ninja
Book 1 – *FREE!!*
Book 2
Book 3

Diary of a Separated Slime – Book 1

Diary of an Iron Golem Guardian – Book 1

The "Skull Kids" Books

A Continuing Diary about the Skull Kids, a group of world-hopping players

Diary of the Skull Kids
Book 1 – *FREE!!*
Book 2
Book 3

The "Fan Series" Books

Continuing Diary Series written by Skeleton Steve *and his fans!* Which one is your favorite?

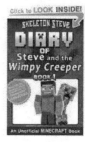 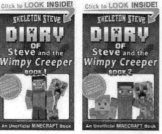 

Diary of Steve and the Wimpy Creeper
Book 1
Book 2
Book 3

Diary of Zombie Steve and Wimpy the Wolf
Book 1 *COMING SOON*

The "Tips and Tricks" Books

Handbooks for Serious Minecraft Players, revealing Secrets and Advice

Skeleton Steve's Secret Tricks and Tips

Skeleton Steve's Top 10 List of Rare Tips

Skeleton Steve's Guide to the
First 12 Things I Do in a New Game

Get these books as for FREE!

(Visit www.SkeletonSteve.com to *learn more*)

Series Collections and Box Sets

Bundles of Skeleton Steve books from the Minecraft Universe. Entire Series in ONE BOOK.

Great Values! Usually 3-4 Books (sometimes more) for almost the price of one!

Skeleton Steve – The Noob Years – Season 1
Skeleton Steve – The Noob Years – Season 2

Diary of a Creeper King – Box Set 1

Diary of a Lone Wolf – Box Set 1

Diary of an Enderman NINJA – Box Set 1

Diary of the Skull Kids – Box Set 1

Steve and the Wimpy Creeper – Box Set 1

Diary of a Teenage Zombie Villager – Box Set 1

Diary of a Chicken Battle Steed – Box Set 1

Sample Pack Bundles

Bundles of Skeleton Steve books from multiple series! New to Skeleton Steve? Check this out!

Great Values! Usually 3-4 Books (sometimes more) for almost the price of one!

Skeleton Steve and the Noob Mobs Sampler Bundle
Book 1 Collection
Book 2 Collection
Book 3 Collection
Book 4 Collection

-

Check out the website
www.SkeletonSteve.com
for more!

Enjoy the Excerpt from...
"Diary of a **Lone Wolf**" Book 1

About the book:

Dakota was a young wolf, happy with his life in a wolf pack in the taiga forest where he was born.

Almost fully-grown, Dakota was fast and loved to run. He had friends, loved his mother, respected his alpha, and had a crush on a young female pack-mate.

But his life was about to change forever when his pack was attacked by *the Glitch*, a mysterious and invincible horde of mobs that appeared and started killing everything in their path!

Now, he was a **lone wolf**. With the help of Skeleton Steve, would he ever belong to another pack again? Would they escape *the Glitch* and warn the rest of Diamodia?

Love Minecraft adventure??

Read on for an Excerpt for the book!

Day 1

So how does a *wolf* tell a story? What should I say, Skeleton Steve?

Oh? Where should I start?

Okay.

So, I guess, my name is *Dakota*. I'm a wolf.

Heh … I already said that. I guess, technically, I'm a *dog* now. No? Doesn't matter?

Skeleton Steve is telling me that I'm a wolf. *Steve* calls me a dog. But I don't understand much about what *Steve* says.

Is this confusing? I'm sorry. Where was I?

Just from … okay, right before.

Well, I guess I can start by telling you about my old pack. My family.

Just a few days before the attack, it was a day like any other.

I woke up in the forest and leapt to my feet! It was a *beautiful* morning. The forest was in shadows of the rising sun, a cool breeze was crisp on my face, and I could smell the woods come alive! Approaching a tall pine tree, I scratched my shoulders on its bark.

All of my pack was waking up around me.

What a great life!

I ran down to the creek, and drank some water. Splashed my face into it. *Cold!* And shook my fur, sending drops of cold mountain water all over before bounding back up the hill.

I guess it's a good time to introduce *the pack*.

My eyes went first to the alpha and his mate. Logan and Moon. Logan was a huge wolf, and he was really nice. He and Moon didn't talk with us very much, but he was a good leader. Logan mostly kept to himself, quiet and strong, and he led us through the mountains day by day whenever we moved.

Right now, we'd spent the last several days hanging out *here*. There were fields full of sheep nearby, and with this nice, flat area, a mountain creek down the hill a bit, and plenty of shade, it was a good clearing to stay in for a while. I was sure we'd move on soon. We always did.

My belly rumbled. We didn't eat yesterday. Today, I knew the alpha would probably send Archie and me to scout out another herd of sheep for the pack to hunt. I was so *fast*, one of the fastest wolves in the pack, and Archie was pretty fast too, so Logan usually sent us out to find the food.

I loved my job! It was great, roaming around with my best bud, running as fast as we could, exploring the mountains all around the clearing where the pack lived. It was only last year when I was finally old enough to be given a job to do. I loved being able to help my family so well.

Taking a big breath of fresh air, I looked around at the rest of the pack waking up and frolicking in the brisk morning.

Over at the edge of the forest were Colin and Arnou. They were the *warriors*, really. We all help each other, and we all have shared tasks given to us by the alpha, but the big and muscular brothers, Colin and Arnou, were really great at fighting, and they were always the first to defend the pack against any mobs that attacked us—the first aside from *Logan the alpha*, that is.

There was my mother, Minsi, one of the older female wolves. I loved my mother. She sat on her own this morning, watching the birds and chewing on a bone.

Running and playing together was the mated pair, Boris and Leloo. Leloo helped raise the cubs (all of the females did, really), and Boris, along with his brother Rolf, were very good at hunting and taking down our prey. The two hunter brothers were very skilled at circling a herd of sheep or other food, and making the animals run whichever way they wanted.

Sitting in the shadow of a couple of pine trees were Maya, and her daughter, Lupe.

Lupe was my age.

She was a beautiful wolf. And smart too. And funny.

I dunno. For some reason, I had a really hard time *talking* to her. Archie joked with me a lot that I should make her my mate, but whenever I walked up to her, whenever I tried to talk to her, my tongue became stupid, I forgot was I wanted to say, and I just embarrassed myself whenever I tried.

It was terrible! Yes, I guess, I really, really liked her. It should have been easy!

Easy just like with Logan and Moon. Logan has been alpha since before I was born, but my mother told me that before he was alpha, when he was younger, he just walked up to Moon one day and *decided* that they were going to be mates.

I don't really understand how that works. Maybe one day I will.

"Hey, dude!" said Archie, running up to see me.

"Oh, hey! Good morning!" I said, sitting in the dirt.

169

Archie was a year older than me, and my best friend. When we were growing up, we always did everything together. And now that we were practically adult wolves (almost), we worked together whenever Logan gave us an assignment.

"You ready?" he said, wagging his tail.

"Ready for what?" I asked.

"Going to look for a herd, of course!" he replied.

"Well, yeah, but Logan hasn't told us to yet."

"I bet he will," Archie said.

Not an hour went by before the massive alpha called on us.

"Dakota! Archie!" he said, his deep voice clear above the rest of the pack, chatting in the morning. We ran up and sat before him.

"Yes, sir?" we said.

"You two explore down in the valley today, see if you can find another herd for us to hunt."

"Right away," I said. Archie acknowledged as well, and we departed our pack's temporary home, flying down the hill as quickly as our speedy wolf feet would take us. With the wind in my face, I dodged around trees, leapt over holes, exploded through the underbrush, and felt great!

When we emerged from the huge, pine forest, I felt the sun warm up my face, and I closed my eyes, lifting my snout up into the sky. Archie popped out of the woods next to me.

"Look at that," Archie said. "Have you ever seen anything so beautiful?"

The sunshine on our faces was very pleasant, and looking down, I could see a huge grassy field, full of red and yellow flowers. Little bunnies hopped around here and there, and in the distance was a group of sheep—mostly white, one grey, one black.

Beautiful. I thought of *Lupe*.

"Awesome," I said. "And hey—there's the sheep over there!"

We returned to the pack and led everyone through the forest back to the colorful and sunny meadow we found.

Soon, we were all working together to keep the sheep in a huddle while Logan, Boris, and Rolf, darted into the group of prey and eventually took them all down. After Logan and Moon had their fill, the rest of us were free to eat what we wanted.

I chomped down on the raw mutton and filled my belly. The sun was high, a gentle breeze blew through the meadow, and I felt warm and happy. Archie ate next to me, and I watched Lupe from afar, dreaming of a day when I would be brave enough to *decide* she was my mate.

Life was good.

Day 2

Today Archie and I went for a swim.

It wasn't necessary to go looking for more food yet, according to the alpha, so we were instructed to stay together, for the most part.

As a pack, we didn't eat every day. But sometimes, I got lucky and found a piece of rotten zombie flesh on the ground after the undead mobs burned up in the morning. Today wasn't one of those days, but it happened *sometimes*.

Anyway, it was fortunate that the mountain creek was just down the hill. Archie and I were able to run down and swim, while the rest of the pack sat around digesting all of the mutton we ate yesterday.

A section of the creek was nice and deep, so my friend and I splashed around and competed to see who could dog-paddle the longest. Archie won most of those times, but I know that I'm *faster* than him on the ground, ha ha.

There was a bit of a commotion around lunchtime when my mother happened upon a skeleton archer that was hiding in the shadows under a large pine tree. She gasped and back-pedaled as the undead creature raised his bow and started firing arrows into our midst.

Arnou was nearby, and responded immediately, with Colin close behind.

As the warrior wolves worked together to flank the skeleton, the mob did get *one* decent shot off, and Colin yelped as an arrow sank into his side. But the two strong wolves lashed out quickly, and were able to latch onto the skeleton's arms and legs, taking him down in no time. Only bones remained.

Colin and Arnou each took a bone, and went back to their business of lounging with the pack.

"Are you okay?" I said to my mother.

"Yes, thank you, Dakota," she said. "I'm glad you were out of the way."

"Oh come on, mom," I said. "I could have taken him."

"I know you could have, sweetie," she replied, and licked my face.

I don't know why the skeleton attacked. Sometimes the mobs attacked us. Sometimes not. Sometimes we (especially Colin and Arnou) attacked *them*. We did *love* zombie meat and skeleton bones, but I've never felt the urge to outright *attack* one of the undead to get it. I knew that if we were patient, we would always find more sheep and get plenty to eat.

Later that day, Archie caught me staring at Lupe, and decided to give me a hard time.

"You should go and *talk* to her, man!" he said, nudging me with his snout in her direction. Lupe noticed the movement, and looked over at us. I saw her beautiful, dark eyes for an instant, and then I turned away.

"Cut it out, man! Jeez!" I shoved him back with my body. "You made her look!"

"So what?" he said. "What's wrong with looking?" He laughed. "Maybe she *should* look. Then something will finally *happen*!"

I stole a glance back to her from the corner of my eye. She had looked away, and was laying in the grass again, looking at the clouds as they rolled by. Usually she hung out around her mother, Leloo, but she was by herself for the moment.

Could I? Did I dare?

"Look, dude," Archie said. "She's by herself. *Go for it!*"

I gulped, and looked back at my friend. I looked around at all of the other pack members. They weren't paying any attention. Just going about their own things.

Padding silently through the grass, I approached. Quiet. Well, not *too* quiet. Didn't want to look like I was sneaking up on her! I just didn't want to look *loud*. Okay, I needed to be a *little* louder.

Snap. Crunch. I made some random noises on the ground as I approached.

176

Jeez, I thought. *I'm being a total weirdo! What am I doing?*

Lupe turned her head to my approach, and when I saw her face, my heart fluttered.

"Hi, Dakota!" she said.

She was happy. Good. I wanted to see her happy. Make her happy. Umm ... if she *wanted* to be happy. Then I'd help her be happy. *What?*

"Oh ... hi," I said. Gulped.

She watched. Smiled. Waited patiently. What would I say? I couldn't really think of anything.

"How's it going?" she asked.

"Good. *Great!*" I said. "*Really* great!"

"That's cool," she replied.

I looked back, and saw Archie watching. He nudged at me with his nose from far away. *Go on*, he said without words.

"Uh," I said, "How are you?"

Lupe smiled and looked back at the clouds.

"Oh, I'm fine, thanks." Her tail gave a little wag.

"So, uh," I said, trying to think of something to talk about. "Did you get plenty of mutton yesterday? Lots to eat? I hope you ate a lot! *I mean*—not that it looks like you eat a lot, or too much. I mean—you're not *fat* or anything; I didn't think you look fat—"

Her face contorted in confusion.

Holy heck! What was I doing?

"Um ... I'm sorry! I'm not calling you fat I just ... uh ..."

Lupe laughed a nervous laugh.

"Ah ... yeah," she said. "I got plenty to eat. Thanks to *you*."

"Um ... me, and *Archie*. We found the sheep."

"Yeah, she said. "I know." She smiled, then watched the clouds.

178

"Yeah," I responded. I watched her, trying to think of something to say that wasn't completely *boneheaded*. After a few moments, she noticed me *staring*, and looked back at me. I looked up to the sky.

Her tail gave a small wag.

"Okay, well," I said, "I guess I'll go see how Archie is doing."

"Oh, really?" she asked. "Well, okay, I guess..."

"Okay," I said. "Well, bye."

"Bye," she said, gave me a smile, then looked back to the clouds she was watching.

I walked back to my friend feeling like an idiot, being careful not to walk like a weirdo.

Later that night, I laid in the grass, watching the stars. As the square moon moved across the sky, I looked at a thousand little pinpricks of light, shining and twinkling far, far away, drifting through space.

Most of the pack was already asleep. I could see Lupe sleeping next to her mom. Archie was sleeping near me, and the rest of the pack kept close together—my mother, the warriors and hunters, Leloo. The alphas slept away from us, a little ways up the hill.

The night was quiet, aside from the occasional zombie moan far in the distance, or the hissing of spiders climbing the trees. I was a little hungry, but tried to ignore my belly.

The stars all looked down at me from the vast, black sky, watching over all of us. So pretty.

Day 3

The morning started like all others.

We woke up and the pack was abuzz with hunger. It would be another scouting day for Archie and me. I ran down to the creek to splash cold water on my face, and found a piece of zombie flesh.

Even though I was hungry, I decided not to eat it. I took the delicious piece of meat in my mouth, careful not to sink my teeth into its sweet and smelly goodness, and brought it to my mom.

"Aw, *thanks*, honey!" she said. "Do you want to split it with me?"

"No, that's okay, mom. You have it," I said.

"But you're probably going to go looking for a herd with Archie today, right? You should take some and have the energy."

"That's alright, mom. I'll eat later."

"Okay, but I'll hang onto half of it in case you change your mind, okay?" She started to eat the zombie meat.

As we expected, Logan called on Archie and I to go out and find another herd of sheep. We happily complied, and ran through the forest for the better part of an hour, seeking out prey for the pack.

It was a warm day, and the breeze in my face felt great! My feet were fast, and the forest smelled good, and I ran like the wind. After a while, I caught the scent of mutton, and led Archie to a small herd of sheep wandering around in dense trees.

"There's our meal ticket!" Archie said. "Let's go back!"

"Let's *do it!*" I said, and we laughed as we sprinted through the woods back to the pack.

After dodging through the trees, leaping over boulders, and running silently through the straights like grey ghosts, we approached the forest clearing where the pack was living.

But something was *wrong*.

As we came down the hill, past enough trees to see the clearing, I smelled a weird smell. Something different that I hadn't smelled before. Something *alien*. And as we approached closer, I heard the sounds of battle!

Zombies moaned and growled. Skeletons clattered. Bows twanged, and arrows whistled through the air. I heard growls and scratches, thumps and crashes. Yelps and cries and raw wolf snarls!

"What the—?" Archie cried, as we ran down to the clearing.

Our pack was *fighting for their lives* against a group of zombies and skeletons!

I couldn't count how many of the undead were down there—the scene was confusing. For some reason, the battle was taking place in *broad daylight*, and the mobs weren't burning up in the sun!

In the chaos before us, I had a very hard time making out who was alive and who was already dead. The alpha was obviously still alive, running to and fro between the undead, striking with power and mainly pulling the attackers off of the other wolves. Moon, I think, was doing the same. Several wolves lay dead. My stomach suddenly turned cold...

CHECK OUT
SKELETONSTEVE.COM
... to CONTINUE READING!

The Amazing Reader List

Thank you SO MUCH to these Readers and Reviewers! Your help in leaving reviews and spreading the word about my books is SO appreciated!

Awesome Reviewers:

MantisFang887 EpicDrago887

ScorpCraft SnailMMS WolfDFang

LegoWarrior70

Liam Burroughs

Ryan / Sean Gallagher

Habblie

Nirupam Bhagawati

SKELETON STEVE

Ethan MJC

Jacky6410 and Oscar

MasterMaker / Kale Aker

Cole

Kelly Nguyen

Ellesea & Ogmoe

K Mc / AlfieMcM

JenaLuv & Boogie

Han-Seon Choi

Danielle M

Oomab

So Cal Family

Daniel Geary Roberts

Jjtaup

Addidks / Creeperking987

D Guz / UltimateSword5

Diary of Steve and the Wimpy Creeper
Book 2

TJ

Xavier Edwards

DrTNT04

UltimateSword5

Mavslam

Ian / CKPA / BlazePlayz

Dana Hartley

Shaojing Li

Mitchell Adam Keith

Emmanuel Bellon

Melissa and Jacob Cross

Wyatt D and daughter

Jung Joo Lee

Dwduck and daughter

Yonael Yonas, the Creeper Tamer (Jesse)

Sarah Levy / shadowslayer1818

Pan

Phillip Wang / Jonathan55123

Ddudeboss

Hartley

Mitchell Adam Keith

L Stoltzman and sons

D4imond minc4rt

Bookworm_29

Tracie / Johnathan

Jeremyee49

Endra07 / Samuel Clemens

And, of course ... Herobrine

(*More are added all the time! Since this is a print version of this book, check the eBook version of the latest books—or the website—to see if your name is in there!*)